The Ants

Sawako Nakayasu

Global Poetics Series

Les Figues Press

The Ants ©2014 Sawako Nakayasu
Cover art by Kenjiro Okazaki

All rights reserved.

The Ants
FIRST EDITION

Text design by Andrew Wessels
Cover design by Chelsea McNay & Andrew Wessels
Copy editors: Lezlie Mayers, Crystal Salas, Genevieve Shifke, Marlan Sigelman, and Emerson Whitney.

ISBN 13: 978-1-934254-54-7
ISBN 10: 1-934254-54-1
Library of Congress Control Number: 2013958198

Les Figues Press thanks its subscribers for their support and readership.
Les Figues Press is a 501c3 organization. Donations are tax-deductible.

Les Figues would like to acknowledge the following individuals for their generosity: Peter Binkow and Johanna Blakley, Lauren Bon, Elena Karina Byrne, Nicholas Karavatos, Coco Owen, and Dr. Robert Wessels.

Les Figues Press titles are available through:
Les Figues Press, http://www.lesfigues.com
Small Press Distribution, http://www.spdbooks.org

Global Poetics Series
GPS-2

LES*FIGUES*
PRESS

Post Office Box 7736
Los Angeles, CA 90007
info@lesfigues.com
www.lesfigues.com

for Eugene

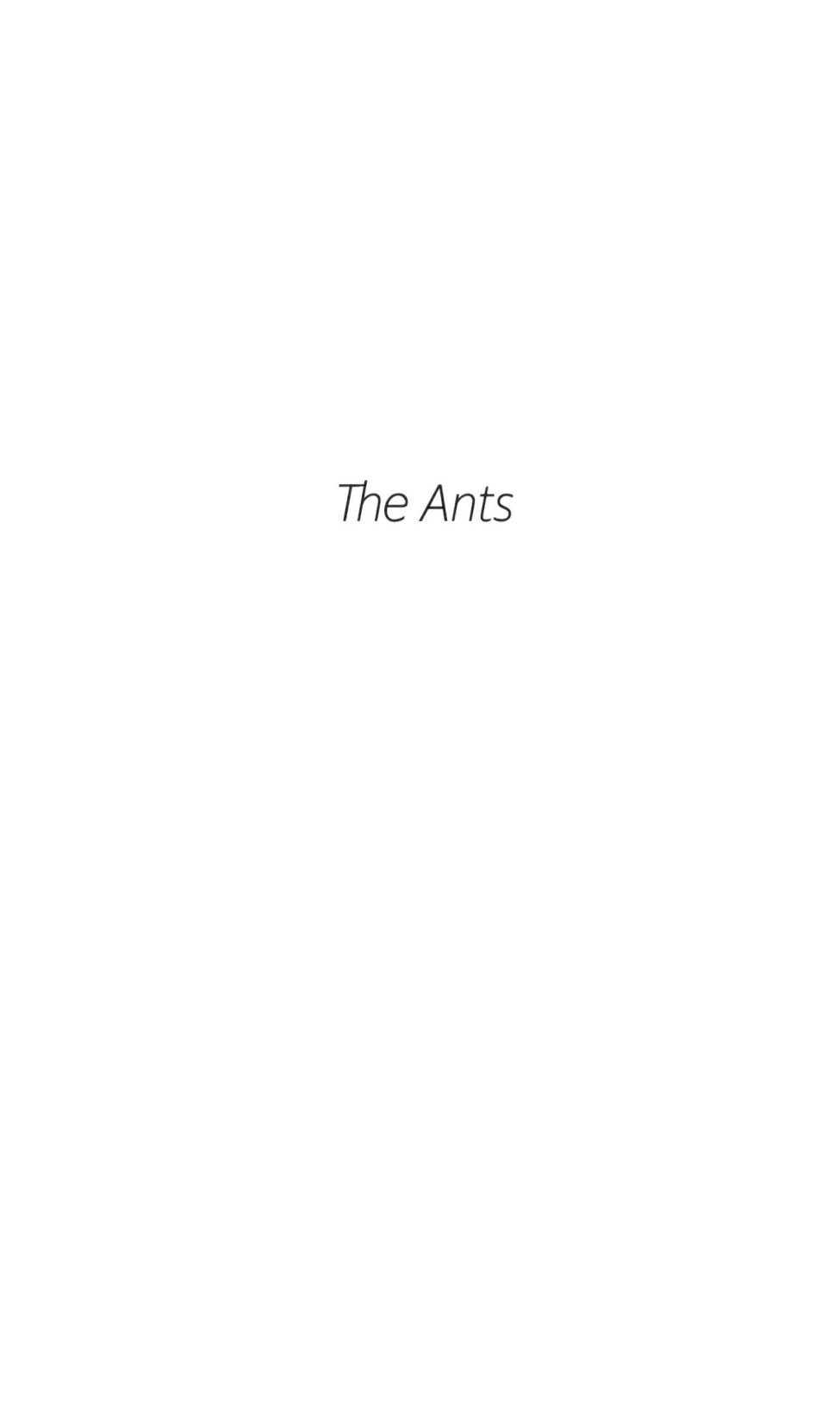

The Ants

We the Heathens

We go to have Chinese for dinner and my friend who is visiting from another planet is horrified (and perhaps a little excited also), until I explain to her that we are having Chinese food, not Chinese people. We go to a place that serves not dumpling soup, which I love, but soup dumpling, with which I am unfamiliar. The soup is actually inside of each dumpling, and everyone develops their own system of eating it. As we poke our chopsticks voraciously into the folds of the Crispy Fried Whole Exploded Fish, which is delicious, it becomes clear to me that we would have no right to be shocked or mortified or outraged or even surprised or upset, should some creature from another planet descend upon the earth, pluck our people off the ground and fry us up, tearing away at our flesh with relish.

My friend Morton, a sweet and gentle man, is sitting quietly beside me with his uneaten hamburger. I don't know how he managed to get himself a hamburger in a Chinese restaurant, but there he sits, and there sits his hamburger, with the top bun off. Morton says he wants live ants on his burger but does not want to go hunting for ants himself, so he is waiting for the ants to come to the burger, at which point he will replace the top bun and eat. I tell him that he will probably have better luck with that outside, and he says that's a good idea, thanks, and goes outside with his hamburger, and that's the last I ever see of him.

An Ant in the Mouth of Madonna Behind Locked Doors

Is there, is there, is there but can't prove it to anyone, is small, is glistening and black, is determined, is hanging on, is at a loss for a good perch, is wet, is blown by the wind when she takes a breath, is happy, is uncertainly happy, is ardent, is devoted, warm and plenty, full of courage, is going to write a Moby Dick-length book about this upon returning, is unsure, is still looking to perch, is unable to see its own feet, is developing a relationship, its first adult relationship, is in a wet place or a hard place, is not strong enough to hang on, not even to the backs of her teeth, is hardly noticed, is tentative, is shy, is timid, is sweet, oh if only it could prove it, is waiting for its chance, is waiting for a big break, is going to show those folks back home, is feeling the slightest bit homesick, is determined to make it, is determined to go down in history, is determined to beat the odds, is casually hoping to make it into the Guinness Book of World Records for the Longest Time Spent in Madonna's Mouth, is an optimist at heart, is fearful in the moment when her breathing gets rough, is shaking, is shaking, is shaken, is having a once-in-a-lifetime experience, is, after all, an ant with a fairly short lifespan, is gay, is not gay, is female, is black, is uncertain, is nothing compared to the giant scale of all the people who surround her, is everything relative to the other organisms inside her mouth, is big-hearted, is open-minded, is sweet, really, all it ever wants is for her to, for her to, oh, and then she comes, and the ant is, and isn't, and is.

Ladybug

I am looking for my friend who promised to meet me on this street at a time that's right about now, except we failed to specify exactly at which part of the block we would meet, and even then it should not be a problem because I know exactly what my friend looks like and yet I am not seeing her at all anywhere on the block. I ask around, to the local shopkeepers, but they haven't seen her either and I look around some more and I still don't see her but fortunately right then she calls and says to look behind me, and I do and I still don't see her, and she says look down, and I do and I still can't find her, and she says she is under that pile of swarming ladybugs right there and I am horrified but she says she is having a good time and that I should come and join her and I walk away and that was the sad end of our friendship.

Girl Talk

We are sitting around the table eating and drinking and exchanging stories about flashers, gropers, underwear thieves, your general assortment of urban perverts. When I tell the story about the man who came up to me and opened up his bag and offered me one of a teeming million wiggling ants in his bag, the whole table goes silent and I am reminded all over again how hard it is to get along with the women in this country.

Battery

We get lost in the desert, lost very lost, and although we aren't going to tell anyone that we can't possibly be any more than two miles from civilization, the fact remains that we are lost very lost in the desert very desert, and the car very car is having a hard very hard very hard time getting started up again, and so we kick it very kick it in its ass very ass and the car is still having a hard very hard time and we are feeling lost all the more lost very lost in this desert very desert, and there is no one around us no no one very around us at all very all and there are birds very birds of which there are many very many, but the birds very birds don't know don't know how to help us and us and us help start the car very car and we are more lost more lost and we need help need very very help need very very help help and there is no no no one around us except if you count count count those ants in the ant hill that is all we have all we have are the ants very ants and then we wire them up yes wire them up yes I said wire wire wire and with the force of all the ants all wired all wired up and then on the count of three we all yell "CHARGE!"

Ant Farm

When I was a small child I wanted an ant farm very much, but never had it, never got my ant farm. I tried to make my own, filling dirt in a jar and gathering all the neighborhood ants and throwing them in there and covering it with plastic wrap and punching holes on top, but somehow it never quite turned into that ant farm I always did want.

Also when I was a small child I was told that the watermelon seed I just swallowed would sprout in my stomach and I would grow a watermelon right inside my body. And that if I didn't get that splinter out of my finger, it would pop out later through my eyeballs. What did happen, however, is that a couple of ants managed to find their way inside, set up their nest, like the ant farm I always wanted, right inside my very own arteries and veins, going up and down the corridors of my circulatory system, riding the blood current, those freeloaders. The ant farm I always wanted.

Now I am disappointed—and isn't this the way it goes—I finally get my ant farm and don't even get to observe it. Not only do I not get much enjoyment out of this, but I also find, or feel, rather, that I am reaching maximum capacity, which is not good. There is not enough room, and yet there is no way for the ants to exit.

What they need is a wound. And so it is that I am forced to call up my friend who owns a gun to come over and shoot me, somewhere harmless like my leg, where it won't kill me, just make a big gushing wound large enough so the ants can get out, and he does, and they do, and now do I miss them.

Colors

I leave the house for a couple of months, and upon my return find that a gang of ants and a gang of cockroaches have been having turf wars in my home. I don't actually see any ants or cockroaches, but I can tell by those little tiny colorful bandanas they have left behind.

Slackers

Back to the ant farm circulating in my body. So we said that we were approaching maximum capacity and that I was going to have my friend shoot me so that all the ants can gush right out of the gaping wound, but not every ant is as simple as all that. They've heard the stories from their older siblings, that once you gush out from an open wound there's no telling what might happen—and so it is, of course, that the smart thing to do is to hang out by the heart, loiter just below the inferior vena cava, hold on to each other in a tight chain so as to resist getting pushed out into the cold harsh world. There are some ants that hold on like this for ages, for all time, burrowed into little nooks, even—hiding out in my heart where they know there is always a home, safe, pounding and ever so warm.

Apple Speed

We have our light years, and they. Their longest unit of time is based on nothing else but. The lifespan of one of their own and. Different colonies may use different varieties of apple, but. The time it takes for a single ant to eat an entire. Apple. The fact of the matter is, working alone makes the task excruciatingly. Slow. Working alone, a single ant is unable to eat the entire. Thus a new replacement ant must. Take over for the old ant at exactly the right. Which means that a number of ant eggs are readied and placed nearby so that when death arrives for the first ant, the most recently born ant can immediately take over the job of the former. In this way, a series of single ants is required in order to consume an entire. And so it goes that an apple speed is the sum of a number of ant-lifetimes, the total amount of time required for the consumption of an entire apple by one hypothetical, long-living ant, and so then the question might go, how many apple speeds does it take to dig this hole, from right here under my feet, straight through the underground and popping back up again over there where you.

Wall

I finally get to meet Matthew for the first time, and so we sit in a café at a little table by the wall and we are facing each other talking but there is a little fruit fly that kind of hovers in the way, near both our faces and the wall. Matthew sort of grabs at it with his hand and slams it against the wall. But you didn't even get the bug, I say. He says I know, it was more of a threat. The next time the bug is over on my half, I wait until it gets close to the wall and slam it directly against the wall with my hand. Nice, he says. And I am thinking that if only he played hockey he would know that it's much better to set up in front of the net and then one-time it, rather than catching the puck first and then taking a shot—but he is already telling me about the woman on the other side of the country that he is distantly, currently, ardently courting.

Training

And so this guy's nice enough to let us use his face for a couple hours, so we quick round up the kid ants, the ones we think are gonna make it, we line them up behind each ear, blow our whistles, we gotta get these ants in shape. I whistle and they sprint across the forehead, touch the other temple, sprint back backwards. Repeat, this time across the eyebrows. All the drills start and end at the ear. I whistle twice and they sprint straight across the cheek, scramble up over the nose, slide down, and keep going clear to the other ear. Repeat, this time going across the bumpy part—the eyes, the bridge of the nose, pick up an eyebrow hair, go all the way to the other ear.

And then—this is where it really gets tricky. After the whistle, go straight to the nostril, get in there and grab a package, a good solid one, working together with one or two ants to bring it out and back to the ear. But when they get inside his nose it makes him sneeze, oh yes it sure does, and they all slide off his face and need to scramble back up to his ears and start all over again, yup this is the tricky part. Now his face trembles slightly and we don't know if we're gonna make it in time. Since everybody dropped their packages in the last commotion, we need to grab them all over again, new ones. It's almost impossible to keep the guy from sneezing, but we work very carefully and then it works out somehow.

And now if that wasn't hard enough. We were saving this for last, but what we really need to work on is the mouth. First you worry about getting in there at all, and then you worry about what is actually going to get brought out from in there. So the whistle blows, but most of the sharp ones know not to sprint out immediately, as there is nothing worse than having to loiter around the edges of a closed mouth waiting for it to open up, which actually makes it less likely that it will open. No, the timing has to be just right, and the ants work very hard on this, working out the rhythm and pacing of all of that which allows for any number of ants to slip inside an open mouth, find some food chunks in the crevices of the teeth, scramble back out before getting closed in, possibly forever, in that deep, dark human hole, oh now don't you get trapped inside there, kids.

Argument

Two humans travel from 'far and great distances,' from a reasonable approximation of what might be called the 'opposite ends of the earth,' and arrive simultaneously in China. Beijing, to be exact. Each begins on one end of what were the original ends of the 'Great Wall of China,' traversing the path atop or along its remains, and meet, face to face, at some perceived midpoint of the wall as determined by their individual paces. Upon arrival, the two humans slowly open their 'mouths,' in a slowness partly necessitated by the fact that their 'mouths' had resolutely and adamantly remained closed for the entire duration of the walk. 'The entire duration.' To get things underway, one 'Starter Ant' leaps out, quickly followed by a few more. A string of ants, with the larger ones clutching tightly to the molars, linked mandibles to hind legs, mandibles to hind legs, shoot forward with the 'Bungee-Maneuver,' hoping to rebound their way back into the safety of the mouth—only to be rudely broken by an 'Opposition String' of ants. The 'Argument' develops. Mid-size ants are propelled forth by the 'Twelve-Ant Double-Helix Spring System.' One lands in the opposing human's mouth, and the team of 'Hurrah Ants' standing by on the 'Hairline Lookout' applauds the great coup. Infuriated, the opposing human 'closes up' and 'turns away.'

Couch

After countless days and nights of living together, a couple decides to get divorced. It takes a little over a few hours of negotiating over their material possessions before they give up and decide to call the ants. She gets on the phone and calls up her ants, likewise he gets up and calls his ants. The ants arrive at 8 a.m. the following Monday, and quickly set to work. Around 4 p.m., the couple returns and enters gingerly, wondering if any progress has been made. While questions still fly about the room as to what will happen to the refrigerator, the records, and the television, they find that the couch has been broken down into small chunks, neat little couch chunks, all thanks to the his and her ant set they had received for their wedding.

A Linear Night

I had never intended to become an artist, but come to think of it, perhaps it can all be traced back to the Great Graphite Shortage of 1979, a dark moment in the history of pencil factories throughout the world, particularly in Japan. Owing to a lack of integrity on the part of the foreman at the Taguchi Pencil Factory in Arakawa, some pencils were temporarily filled with crushed ants instead of crushed graphite. The internal secretions of the ant were a handy replacement for the clay commonly used to bind the graphite, the foreman had reasoned. To be sure, they had called in the scientists to ensure that the pencils would be filled with just the right density of ant in order to achieve a result very close to the HB (#2) pencil.

Who could have guessed why my lines were coming out funny. I gave up on writing characters in their originally intended manner and just let the lines do as they would. In spite of criticism from schoolteachers, I did know, at that early age, that I was not the only force (or weakness, as some would say) involved in the formation of these convoluted lines. It's just that at the time, most people were speaking of Martians and Muses as common sources of artful thinking, and I hadn't ever before heard about the ant incident at the Taguchi Pencil Factory, but I also remember now, come to think of it, something funny about the way those lines erased, something about the way the pencil particles never blended very well with the pink eraser particles, something I only barely noticed as I wiped my desk clean with those small, once-innocent hands of mine.

Capture the Flag

Anywhere inside of a human being is safe, anywhere outside is not.

Some ants refuse to play, which unfortunately leaves them in a permanently unsafe state. The more evolved an ant, the more attuned it is to the emotional and social weather patterns of humans, preying on that moment of unexpected rudeness and the consequent open jaw of the recipient, through which it may enter and be safe, safe as ever.

And yet how rude or polite was that, in the larger context of ant-human relations?

Harsh Edit

My editor is a bit old-fashioned, and still likes to come over to my house to pick up manuscripts. Except that my printer is broken right now, so what ends up happening is that he shows up and we do a file transfer and that way there is still some remnant of that handing-over of the manuscript, which makes him very happy. None of this matters all that much, and neither does the fact that every time he comes over I discover something new about him. We've known each other for many years now, so that amounts to a lot of information.

This last visit I get a little careless, however, and leave my ant out while I go to the bathroom. When I come out, much to my surprise, I find that he has edited my ant, without even asking. Now on the one hand I am of course quite shocked and outraged by this gesture, but then on the other hand I think that maybe the ant looks cute this way, with shorter front legs and the mandibles filed down, but I will have to wait until my editor goes home so that I can talk candidly with the ant and figure out what is truly best for all of us involved.

Curling

And so I have come to note that my aging parents have begun to shift their actions somewhat slightly, just barely perceptibly leaning towards a direction which might make things a little easier for me during the difficult moment of their departure.

And so today I have come to take notice of a colony of ants, afflicted by what might possibly be some sort of ant-plague. It appears that many of the ants have stopped moving, but as I advance my face closer to the ants, and as my own vision slows down, I begin to see that many of these ants are in fact still moving in place, their motion turning inward, their surfaces and extremities curling into the center and I share for a moment the anticipation of those stronger ant limbs that will soon come around to lift and carry, lift and carry.

Decay

The great desire is to get inside of it—the poem, the painting, the movie, the music.

An ant, perceiving itself to have failed to get *in* anywhere, takes one brave leap off a cliff, thereby making its last and final attempt to get into something, anything, anyhow.

On its way down, or perhaps at the moment it lands (neither of us are quite sure which), it makes an undeniable percussive sound as its body breaks, pops, and for the entire duration of the decay of this sound, it is as inside as it can get, there, inside that sound, however short-lived, who cares if it is witnessed or not.

Carrot Cake

I make a carrot cake for the first time, eat a little bit before going to bed, and forget to put it away. It's not bad for a first attempt, I tell myself as I fall asleep. In the middle of the night, an ant on a reconnaissance mission stumbles across the leftover carrot cake, and by the following morning the whole colony has descended upon it. All of this sounds normal enough so far, but it turns out that this particular colony of ants is of the gypsy variety with no fixed domicile, and has decided to take on the carrot cake as its new home. So these ants are not eating my carrot cake, but living in it, using it as their headquarters as they shuffle in and out and to and fro and out and about, hunting for food in the usual ant-like manner. It was only last night that I had thought my carrot cake decent enough, and yet here I am now, facing the unbearable fact that not only can I no longer eat my own carrot cake, but that even the ants, insultingly enough, did not find it good enough to eat, and not only that but here it is in front of me, the ant farm I had always longed for, and yet I can't see it, can't see through the metal pan, the ant farm that I always wanted.

Desert Ant

Says "and" with every step, so that it sounds like this: "and and and and and and and and and and and," and so on. By the time I make my way to the same desert, I have been collecting and carrying an accumulation of nouns over the past, oh I don't know how many days, and so I insert them in between the steps of the ant. Cilantro, tennis, phone, hand. Needle, rock, hair. Mingus. Monk. Mouth. I have been ignoring the dirty looks the ant keeps giving me, but finally I cave in, which means I stop to listen carefully. I am informed that I have thrown off the rhythm of "and and and and and." I am informed that this shall not continue. I am given several options. I choose Monk, so for a while we do "Monk and Monk and Monk and Monk and Monk and Monk and Monk." I thought we were doing okay, but before I know it the ant is out of sight, and then before I know it, the ant has made a decision, and then before I know it, the ant is in my mouth, and mouth, and mouth, and mouth, and mouth, and mouth, and mouth.

Aggregate Heat

An accumulation of very small things: for example, the heat transmitted from let's say an ant in every instance of its putting down what is at the very end of one of six appendages or legs, shall we call them feet for the time being, as it makes its way across the surface of an open newspaper—except that only in the instances where an ant foot touches the black ink of a newspaper shall the heat qualify to be measured and included in the overall aggregate, in this case the Ant Heat Transmission with the Ink Provision.

We are on our merry way to coming up with a very small but very lovely number, when a fight breaks out in the household. Two human voices are yelling at each other in the other room, which means that the dog goes crazy, because the dog goes crazy whenever humans get in a fight, but only when they are really fighting. We've tried this before, pretend-fighting, where the dog just looks on with mild bemusement or disinterest, and so it is that we are such bad actors that we can't even fool our dog. But when the fighting is real and the dog goes crazy, it runs about all over the house. The newspaper was on the floor, and the dog only stepped on just a small corner of it, but it is enough to alarm the ant walking atop it, and now the ant goes crazy.

Or rather, it starts running, all six appendages working together for the common purpose of I don't know what. Panic, perhaps. So the number of steps taken by the ant per second increases, but this also means that the ant makes its way off the paper as quickly as it possibly can. Now we are unsure if the aggregate measure of heat is larger in this case, the case that happened, or if it would have been greater had the ant stayed calmly meandering the black and white splotches on the newspaper on the floor.

Halloween

Is notorious for its horrible rush hour traffic, but we forget about this every year and get stuck in the thick of it. To our credit, though, we also take things one step further every year, and this year we are all ants. I mean real ants—ant-scale, ant-size, anty-ants in your underpants, and it's no longer about the rush hour traffic of mere cars, oh no, our rush hour is about the traffic of ants, of course. There is candy over here and candy over there, our home is over here and everyone's out on street level, in line in one of a maxed-out number of trails, something like twenty or thirty—those five-lane freeways are for humans.

Our ant-trail rules have changed, however. It's a new age, and where it once was okay to touch each other, by chance or on purpose, we've inherited something from the humans and now are not supposed to touch, ever. If you do touch it's called an accident and you have to call the authorities and the insurance people and no one has time for this, it's a big mess. There's no safety in direct contact. And yet look at that speeding kid over there, I can't bear to watch it, and HEY! I said don't touch me, and don't touch me there, what kind of ant do you think I am?

Happy Holidays

A cat or dog of unknown origin is approaching quickly. You have been instructed not to pet it. These instructions have come from someone somewhere many years ago and are just now resurfacing out of the recesses of your memory. As events over the course of this loaded one- or two-minute moment unfold, the cat or dog produces out of its mouth not a full set of menacing teeth, but a single, living ant. And is this an offering, salutation, or insult. Or Christmas.

Fear of Cold

For some reason, I am stranded in an extremely cold environment without my coat, and start to worry if my life is in danger. After what seems like an adequate amount of suffering has taken place, I am fortunate enough to find a house, into which I break in and find a marginal amount of relief. There is nothing at all in the house, there is no power of any kind, and there is a large pile of dead ants near the bathroom door. I am a direct descendant not of MacGyver but his old-fashioned sister, and so I end up using my Other-MacGyver skills to weave a blanket out of the dead ants, which I finish as quickly as I can, and then throw over my body, begging it to bring me warmth. What happens is that I am so repulsed by the fact of having a blanket of ants covering my body that I quickly grow both sick and intensely anxious about the situation, from which all of the nervous energy causes the blood cells in my body to vibrate rapidly until I am quite warm, and stay warm until the weather goes warm and I am saved from dying.

Ant Intrusion 1

A gun is jumped on many counts, the sprinter gets called back to the starting line, the car lurches, an unripe cantaloupe tastes like cucumber, the snow is not soft enough or enough enough, the bathwater is lukewarm, the fire too small, the marshmallow on fire, the meat raw, the brownies gooey, the sun still a healthy distance from the horizon, the computer still starting up, the fortress not yet fortified, the gas still pouring, the road unpaved, the post office line too long, the gum still wrapped, the lens cap still on, the bird still mid-flight, the boy still working his way, slowly, glacier-like, trying to catch up to some hemisphere of thought or kiss or an estimated Bosnian scale of time, the woman is WAITING PATIENTLY! WAITING PATIENTLY! WAITING PATIENTLY! when it finally happens, an arrival, destination, a long-awaited collision of intention, and all appropriate animate creatures are making their way to their respective places, when an ant, one ant, stands up and raises a single ant hand.

The Cannibal

Has made his latest killing, he sits down with his fork and special knife, all excited about digging into the flesh, the chewy stomach, the long intestines. When he bites into an intestine, he is startled to find it stuffed with live, undigested ants, and has no idea what to make of this new and bewildering situation.

No Collective

Believing themselves to be quite progressive for their species, a group of ants gets together and decides to form a collective. They gather the necessary documentation, fill out all the proper information in the correct little boxes, get photos taken in the right size and dimensions and angle, and step precisely through every single hoop required of them to become an officially recognized collective.

Their application is denied, however, on the grounds that ants are an inherently collective species, and this designation would be redundant and downright unnecessary.

One ant is so upset by this verdict that it begins to cry, thereby forging a breach in the collective emotional unity of the group. This very breach, however, makes the officer falter, reconsider for a brief moment, entertain the possibility of a radical change of heart, but this very possibility of a change in the officer's heart makes the ant's tears dry up, which lands them all back at their original, inherently collective state, and that's the end of that story.

Anewal

A fly and a cow meet up in the center of a storm. It could be love—love! But more likely it is the natural inclination of all creatures, faced with the burden of immediate chaos and fear, to grasp for the familiar, to reach out and hang on. Never mind that the great physical force of this thing called storm is most likely the reason for this haphazard encounter between fly and cow.

From the perspective of the fly and the cow: the present circumstances of storm create a meeting which lasts barely half a moment, in a quick breath of physical contact. The fly, skimming the surface of the cow's torso, finds therein an illusion of comfort, safety, and shelter from the tempest, however short-lived such refuge may be. Meanwhile the cow is temporarily relieved from the throes of a helpless itch, as the fly scrapes by and with its body provides a welcome scratch. All of the above events allow both parties to experience each other quite differently from their everyday relationship, the stinkier one, involving the dung of the cow and the bouncy loitering of the fly, the typical swish of the cow tail batting lazily at the fly, a lopsided relationship that we all thought was never ever ever going to change.

Parade

Today is a unique holiday, commemorated by a parade of black, four-legged stools going down the closed-off street. All the neighborhood ants come out to take a look, most of whom take a very critical stance.

Hazing

Takes place in several parts of the house at once. Each ant is instructed to choose a light bulb, and to stay there as long as possible. The real test comes when the human inhabitants come home and start turning on the lights. The clever ants who can read numbers have chosen bulbs with lower wattage, but most ants are not as literate as all that. The humans proceed to make their dinner using wholesome, all-organic ingredients. All the ants hold their breath.

Sufficient Gravity 1 (Wind)

What people don't pay much attention to is the fact that during the summer, there are an infinite number of festivities and contests that take place throughout the land over, but for today's installment we're going to be featuring summer at Coney Island, live from under our feet.

A large number of ants and one human.

In the name of fairness, the ants are allowed only to compete against other ants of the same class, as determined by volume. This is calculated by the displacement method, with a small graduated cylinder half-filled with water. Some ants never break through the surface tension of the water and thus are unable to get measured, which is the first method of elimination.

One class at a time, the ants line up and take their places upon a grid, with sufficient room surrounding each ant body. At the sound of the whistle, each ant releases as much personal gravity as is antly possible, at the same time that a person blows, as hard as is humanly possible, right over the line of ants. The single last ant who remains, while all the others have been blown away, is the winner.

At the end of the day, there is a complicated algorithm that determines which ant from which class is the true champion of the entire contest, and often, it just so happens to be that the winner is an unsuspecting ant from the main isle of Japan, as it also happens to be that the only witnesses to the whole event are the delicate flowers, who look on with bemusement at the thought.

Sufficient Gravity 2 (Slide)

A place where ants, small ants, can go to have fun—some refer to this as the New Kindergarten for Small Ants. The main attraction is an ant-sized slide, where ants can slide down one by one. The great thing about this slide is that it is calibrated to the exact pitch of the sound made by an ant as it slides down, and so as the ant goes downward, making a sound that increases in inverse proportion to the intensity of sound made by the slide, at the exact point which corresponds to the half-life of the decay of the sound of the slide, the ant feels a little pop. Now this moment of pleasure is available only to those ants of the correct ant-weight—not too light and not too heavy—and this, ladies and gentlemen of all ants and persuasions, is at the root of many of our contemporary social ailments, is it not.

Sufficient Gravity 3 (The Surface Tension Challenge)

Things have evolved as far as this. Once every summer in a nondescript beach town in Southern California, a contest is held. On a smooth, very smooth surface, a puddle, very large puddle is formed. Local ants are invited to the puddle, all with the awareness that the ant who breaks the surface tension, and thus the puddle, shall be the winner of a brand-new Chrysler Crossfire Limited. The task looks easy enough that it lures a few ants to jump on first, not realizing the inadequacy of their body mass until it is too late. More ants then pile on quickly, so that the judges are forced to keep a sharp lookout in order to correctly identify the ant that breaks the water surface. When the number of ants atop the puddle starts approaching critical mass, the ants grow restless and the whole puddle quivers.

The puddle attracts quite a bit of attention, and ants, whole colonies of ambitious ants and poor ants and lonely ants with nothing to do, seeking a little friendly jostling, hopeful ants, and soon even the random passerby ants with no ambition whatsoever have joined in on the action, having been lured in by all the ongoing excitement. It is just this kind of unambitious ant who finally ends, by winning, this mad contest of jostling ant matter, and is presented with the car. At which point the ants are now returned to their senses, reminded that this game was a human invention after all, the car a human-scale car.

The winning ant is now faced with the Herculean task of gathering enough fellow ants to band together and form a massive huddle, a complex collective large enough with which to operate the car. A pair of ants nearby loiter around the butt of a not-quite-extinguished cigarette, taking turns inhaling, and exhaling statements about how overrated winning is.

Cavities

Clearly this is all because of my parents, I used to resent them for it but now perhaps it is all finally okay, all of it happening not because they failed to institute good habits of oral hygiene back when I was a little kid, but more because I was deprived of the chance to own any pets as I was growing up—how I would have loved to feed, walk, and lavish my attention on some breed of dog, or even a cat, or even a rodent or fish—but there were absolutely no pets, none whatsoever, in my youth and subsequent thereafter. They say this about one's formative years, that they mold you in certain shapes that are difficult to later modify—in my case it is my teeth they have molded—and so then who can blame me when the pets come to me, just arrive without my even noticing, just show up oh-so-subtly and find a way to take care of themselves, so that now I am with pet and don't even have to do any work to that end, which is fortunate since my lonely childhood certainly did nothing to prepare me for this. The ants in my teeth are excellent burrowers, they have been digging in for a while now, have made a home for themselves within the smooth corridors of my teeth. They have finally found their home and I have finally found my pets, and this must be what it feels like when the right match is made, such is the feeling of rightness that comes over me whenever I think about my pets or feel something ever so gently grazing my tongue.

Swimming in the Presence of Lurid Opposition

Summer camp, swim class, Tokyo, a group of no more than twenty ants all donning their respective swimming caps, some with images of their favorite anime characters printed on the fabric. Forward progression, assisted by a rhythmic movement of ant limbs, just like the instructor instructed, forward forward progress, forward forward progress. The slowness, agonizing slowness of such poor swimmers, these ants, most likely in the beginner class for sad ants with little ability. And then the However, the Big But, the Truth that reveals itself only after zooming out and away from what used to be a close-up shot of ants in an unusually colored swimming pool, such as red or green or pale fuchsia or celadon, the distance revealing the inherent difficulty of making a swimming pool out of a still-wet oil painting, the artist and brush hovering nearby like the evil clouds that they are.

Ants in the Wind

It's that time of year again, and the ants are filling the air, both the physical air as well as the radio and TV airwaves, not to mention the internet. I can't take two steps in any direction without being accosted by an hourly-updated regional chart of the current ant density levels, which are climbing at exponential rates right in front of my eyes. When I was a child it never went above 30% or so, but this year we have hit an all-time high of 72% ant saturation. I believe it, too, because I look out the window and can see them. Or rather, I can not see very well through them, and this is how I know of their presence, fogging up vision throughout the world over.

Meanwhile, my cousin has made a great living for himself in an industry that happens to profit from natural disasters and mild calamities, and it just so happens that in recent years his business of selling ant filters and inhalation-prevention masks has done quite well. He slips me some free software that filters ant reports out of my computer so that I can get back to work.

Little beknownst to me and everyone else, the ants themselves have been apprehensive about this time of year as well, as it represents the true test of their entire winter of underground training. They have studied countless tutorials, textbooks, videotapes, DVDs, podcasts, everything but the real thing, all invested in the sole purpose of helping to train young ants to prepare for the ride up (which can be quite lovely if caught on the back of a bird), as well as the inescapably treacherous way down. The young ants have undergone numerous visualization exercises in navigating the wind currents, as well as recognition drills so that they know what to avoid (humans, cars, buses, lampposts, spider webs, ocean) and what is safe to encounter (trees, cowhide, corn, sand dune). A large plate of partially chewed strawberry shortcake is provisionally safe (and even pleasant), but one must remain keenly aware of the nearby presence of humans. As the wind sweeps her children away, one mother ant worries herself sick, hoping that she has trained them all properly to use their good judgment, to defend themselves from the harshness of the world that is so anxiously preparing for their arrival.

Watch

Having one day heard the tale of Tehching Hsieh and his year-long Cage Piece, in which the artist confined himself inside a wooden cage for the duration of a year, the ant feels great relief to learn of a kindred spirit, at least one other being out there who might possibly know how this feels. That old second hand is relentless, after all. The ant has a total of two options, three if you count the option which combines the first two.

Option #1 is colloquially referred to as the Jump Rope method, highly valued for the 59 seconds of rest and relaxation offered within the bounds of every single minute. On the other hand, like a Little League right fielder, the long wait between moments of action carries with it the dangers of a wandering imagination, lack of attention, and straying vision, all of which could lead to serious injury and loss, should the second hand arrive at an inopportune moment.

Option #2, the Walk Behind method, inspired by Yoko Ono's film, "Bottoms" (which was later commemorated in a Swatch watch), in which a camera follows the bare, walking bottoms of a series of celebrities, is quite contrary to Option #1, involving a continuous forward motion reminiscent of that observed in domesticated hamsters. On a circular walking path with a 1-cm radius, covering six degrees of circle per second, the ant follows the second hand consistently and without fail. It is quick to master the minor variation of steps required to traverse the occasional minute and hour hands, and is eventually even reminded of bygone days foraging with the colony, marching along at a regular pace.

The Combination method is developed later on as the legs on the ant begin to falter, with the legs on the left side gaining about 30% more muscle than those on the right, with the ant approaching the brink of exhaustion and collapse, even after the development of a walking-backwards system that relieves the accrual of muscular imbalance between the right and left sides of the body. Such a method combines all the long-term benefits of the Walk Behind method, which allows for long-lasting stability and certainty, with the repose offered by the Jump Rope method. The successful implementation of this method involves accumulating enough tiredness during the duration of the Walk Behind method, so as to enter the Jump Rope method with a sleep so deep that one is able to jump over the approaching second hand while hardly disturbing its sleep, in fact continuing right on, as can be attested to by the continuity of the dream therein experienced. The Combination method has its dangers, however, and one is advised to try it only after much experience and familiarity with the Jump Rope method has been achieved.

In fact it is the invention of this, the Combination method, which allows the ant to live well over the 20-day estimate (according to the myrmecologists), until one day I wake up and get ready for work as usual, and when I put on my watch, I see that the ant has developed a new system altogether, and I exchange a few quick words with it as I walk out the door.

What Is an Ant Getting Washed with the Rice?

A vision problem, as in:

The colored thunder of other grains causes a sound just rollickingly wide enough to obscure its vision, and as it, ant, tumbles clockwise alongside the masses of grains and grains of rice, white very white, very much unlike itself, more grains than there ever were ants, and as its vision goes, flies over and across the brink, the milky flood overtaking the clear, overtaking the calm before the flood, ant struggling to reach back with its vision to a moment just before this torrent of chaos—a moment of itself flooding out of its resting position, a single chance to see the world outside of the bag, blinded by the light from above, aching to follow the scent of an onion, passing a bottle, standing in a position, I believe, called still, there beyond, glimpsing unknown glossy yellow objects and a puddle of sauce spilled twelve minutes ago and a crumb, O glorious crumb, and that clear piece of Tupperware on the bottom of which lies another ant, which is in an equally problematic predicament, one that is neither inside nor outside, above or below, but firmly embedded within the plastic of the plastic.

Manifold Destinies

Two ants set out at the same time—one on the tip of my right hand, one on my left—to find out if they were meant for each other, a match made in heaven, star-crossed ants, or none of the above. Everything is within a manageable distance, there is plenty of time, and it would be all too simple, if, for example, I were to lay myself flat on my back, naked, in an empty room with nothing sweet anywhere in the vicinity.

But nothing is as easy as all that in this so-called real world, and since I do have my own life to live, I do just that. I put on clothes, sit in chairs, respond to e-mails. Eat and make phone calls. The ants are doing their thing. I eat again. They continue to try to find each other. I drive to the store. Meet friends. Buy stuff. At some point in the day, time will run out, or an ant will fall off, and it could very well possibly be that as close as they ever got to each other was my torso, one of them circling my front side, the other making endless loops and loops around my lower back.

Ant Liberation

A minor sub-swarm of freethinking and over-educated ants originally from Yorba Linda, California, rally together and decide that they want to be the ones to walk in the sun, that they will take it upon themselves to attain a better life for freethinking ants everywhere, effective immediately.

Using the pretense of a reconnaissance mission gone wrong in order to escape the clutches of the Queen, the ants embark upon a study trip to the Salk Institute in San Diego, California, an institute for biological studies designed by the architect Louis Kahn at the behest of Dr. Jonas Salk, inventor of the polio vaccine. They study the unfinished concrete with its exposed joints, take notes on the adjustable partitions, the wooden shutters of teak, and the corridors of light filtering through the arcade. They argue over whether the formwork markings are best left exposed or not. The next day they repeat the process at the Nobu Hotel Caesar's Palace in Las Vegas, followed by Arches National Park in Utah.

The study is conducted over a period of many days and nights, during which time they also carefully observe and conduct structural analyses of lawn mowers, spider webs, swimming pools, garbage piles, financial trade towers, aspen trees, and the like. We're overthinking it, says one of the freethinking ants, as the group enters yet another huddle, crouched atop an ice floe on a lake of snowmelt in the Rocky Mountains. At last agreeing on the fact that their thinking and note-taking and analyzing activities are not producing the desired results, they resort to following none other than their own ant intuitions, rather than trying to emulate humans with their notebooks and calculators and writing implements. One of the ants is disappointed, but is peer-pressured into silence.

So they go and go and go, across the Central Plains and over the Driftless Area, from the Delmarva Peninsula to Cajun Country and back up to the Inland Empire, through dirt, grass, office buildings and private schools, until one day they find themselves in a lovely pile of medium-fine woodchip, replete with passageways, dead ends, multiple entries and exits, all in a pleasantly malleable yet solid material medium—in other words, everything a freethinking ant could ever hope to find in a home.

There is no need for discussion—the ants move in immediately with minimum effort, happy as a group of freethinking ants could ever hope to be. Soon enough they are all settled in, there are lovely shafts of light that shine warmly down upon them from various directions, and at night they sleep with the smug, peaceful feeling of superiority over every other average ant in its sadly average anthill, until the next day when I discover ants in my hamster cage, tell my mom about it, and she promptly freaks out and empties all the contents of the cage in the backyard as I remove a single ant from my hamster's left ear.

Sign

Look at all those years upon years of so-called civilization and enlightenment and industrialization and this is where it has brought us. Are we any smarter? No. Are we any happier? No. Are we any prettier? No. No. None of the promises came true, and all we have to show for anything is that we can now sign in to all our favorite high-security locales using an ant proxy that sits behind in the liquid of the computer monitor, and this is the truest sign of bratwurst or frog legs or pro-wrestling, oh I just can't say it, that mythical p-word that means that we are somehow doing better than we were before.

Billboard

Everyone keeps asking why I stare so intently at that billboard over there. It is true that in the time it took for me to come all the way to this side of the street, a fair distance from the billboard itself, the circumstances have probably changed, but last time I was over there I noticed an ant running up and down and all around the surface of the billboard. Due to social upheaval in his home and native land, this ant has been uprooted from home, torn away from his wife and children, tossed into a random urban environment such as New York City, and has spent the last many moons fending for himself in this harsh and foreign metropolis.

The reason I keep staring is because the entire surface of this particular giant billboard is filled with the enormous picture of another ant. The ant of whom I speak has recognized this enormous picture as his long-lost wife, and has made a special leap into the second dimension, overcoming the scales of distance and time by frantically running across her body, touching her here, there, again, and more over there, sending his love through the paper and ink and over the years through this frantic and contained marathon, covering vast distances across the surface of the billboard, such that he sees and feels nothing but his wife, his wife, his lovely and billboarded wife.

Box with Arms and Butterflies

A large box with many arms reaching out of just as many holes in the box. The arms reach out and grab butterflies, depositing them back in the box. The butterflies go out the holes, some go so far as to fly away forever, while some get grabbed and returned to the box. The arms look like they just might try to leave the box as well, if they only had bodies to take along.

Chinese Ants on the Wall

The Changcheng. Two ants start on opposite ends, one on the Shanhai Pass and the other at Lop Nur. They each ant-intuit the beginning moment and set out at the exact same time.

Seasons pass. The ants walk towards each other. With summer comes the added danger of Tourist Trampling, and it becomes necessary to walk faster, break into a run at times, in order to avoid the steady onslaught of giant tourist feet marching across. In the midst of one of these summer tramples are two female human vendors—one from the China side and one from the Mongolia side. They are in the cattiest of fights over their individual claims on the same innocent tourist who they believe will eventually buy some of their goods, if followed and encouraged persistently enough.

Their fight is getting very nasty and they are soon on the brink of trying to throw each other off the wall when one of the ants passes by with such force of intention that everyone is drawn to pause. Now these women know about force and intention—they have spent their lives climbing up and down and all across what is known to many as the Great Wall of China chasing after tourists and fighting cracked tooth and broken nail over the possible potential $3 that they may or may not receive in exchange for one of their many tourist offerings including a can of Chairman Mao's Shit, and so they recognize intention when they see it. The passing ant of epic intentions pays no mind to the two women who have now stopped bickering. It in fact does not notice them beyond the fact that they are connected to four more shoes to be dodged, which have thankfully stopped moving, hence improving the ant's ability to estimate the path of least obstruction. The two women in question, neither of whom have yet to make a sale today, have no choice but to acknowledge this great force behind this small creature—they are humbled beyond themselves and find it impossible to continue any further in this line of business.

Old-Fashioned Messenger Ants

Listen: these two devices are the ears with which the two pianos can hear the sounds upon which they base their improvisational decisions as they play alongside two human musicians, who both hear the old-fashioned way (point to both ears).

At not the same time, the ears of an ant are stretched out so that it might hear all the better. A message is conveyed to the now open-eared ant, before it takes a brave leap into some Al Green Chile Stew, made lovingly to be eaten before the arrival of some Barry White Cheesecake.

All are seated around the dinner table. According to an old French tradition, one lucky bowl contains the stew with the old-fashioned messenger ant inside. Said ant floats up onto the spoon in the shadows of some chilies and potatoes and meat, cruises down the throat, into the stomach, and then—after gathering its bearings, rears back just a little before taking a great internal leap, the greatest single feat of its very short ant-lifetime, lands up high on the organ above, where it takes a deep, slow, tender ant-bite out of my heart, that was my heart.

The Ant on the Ship Coming Towards Me

Is, by default, also coming towards me, and has been doing so for as long as it can remember. Without having ever met me or having any concept of what 'me' might be. And in fact I am not really me, I am a sugar cube in the middle of the ocean and the boat is a boat-jacked boat, and now what kind of wussy boat is going to get taken over by an ant. Or, for example, penguins.

Ants Preparing to Catch

Only those deemed fast enough are allowed to play, considering that the ball is already in the air and the collective must make a very quick decision as to whether they will group up first, then move to the correct position, or gather in the correct position first and then group up, but the ball is already descending and some ants won't make it, but those who are close enough get together at superior ant speed, form at first a round mass, until someone calls the error and they rearrange into the shape of a bowl, a thick bowl, but then the ant in the middle at the very bottom of the bowl starts crying in fear and asks to be transferred to the rim, as if there was time for such requests to make it through the system, as if there was time to consider—

Ant Shoes

Are very small, and are typically worn by the most sheltered of ants, and even then only for the first few days of its life, and even then only until it gets ridiculed by all the other ants, at which point it develops, slightly belatedly, a brand-new sense of self-aware shame, and consequently makes the direct connection between its shoes and its embarrassing social status, at which point it is too late and the ant will never live down the fact that it once wore shoes, much like that boy, Scott, who peed his pants one day in kindergarten, many many years ago but I still remember, oh yes I do.

Antennae

One day we realize we are in desperate need of an antenna. There is all of one temp agency open today on this fine particular Sunday in this splendid European city, and the only people they have to spare today are ants, and the only ants available on this day are blue. They are the ants that were cut in the final round of some long-ago, Busby Berkeley auditions, these blue, non-Busby Berkeley ants—washed up, beached, past their ant prime, out of the ant light.

Out of the ant light, and-and-and drowsy, blue and vaguely willing, these ants are summoned, awakened, sent back out, such mercenary temps, and-and-and they show up, flex, combine into formation, ant upon ant upon ant, and-and-and into this half-present, half-prepared moment, under a tense interlude of light they fit together all luminous, upright, with tilt, thank you, antennae, of, of ants.

Progress

One year ago today, a video camera was released to the public, a camera resulting from years and years of development by a pair of French engineers, having been fine-tuned to such a degree that it can capture the kissing of a pair of ants, mandible to mandible, from a great enough distance so as not to disturb them.

Today, however, the true test of academic excellence in our children is entirely dependent upon their ability to measure the heat transfer in an ant kiss, which will be exhibited at this year's International Junior Insect Olympics, which is something akin to a science fair for the young insect-inclined minds of the world. Who will go home with the gold medal this year? Which Asian country is showing the greatest promise in its youth? A controversy breaks out when a group of Americans from somewhere with a low-literacy, high-bravado rate pulls up to the event with their own version of the Ant Kiss Project, involving genetically mutated Hummer-sized ants. Oh you ain't leavin' our children behind just yet, insist their parents. Just you wait and see.

Large

Once upon a time, as in today, and place, as in China, there exists an ant—who for unknown reasons grows to be extraordinarily large—who dreams of moving to the United States, or anywhere, where the ants are supposedly bigger, if only there existed a suitable means of transport—who dreams of going to the Olympics in some foreign country, not so much out of a desire to compete athletically (all that attention and pressure would be much too much), but only because it would involve a ticket out of this place, to anywhere but here—who keeps growing bigger still, big enough, in fact, so as to one day be able to straddle large bodies of water, so that it might, for example, keep a few legs in China, one or two in Korea, and then with a stretch, land each of the front legs on a Japanese island or two, the impact of which causes a more-than-minor earthquake, spreading fear and panic throughout the land, drawing mean glances from the local normal-sized ants of Japan, Korea, and China, none of whom are aware that oversized, gigantic ants are the loneliest ants of all.

Art Project

I am observing an ant trail from the tenth floor of a building, and photograph the exact same frame, once per second, sixty times, in order to have an accumulated minute of ants. Later, much later, I go back to the same exact spot where the ants once were, and place a grain of rice in the exact location of each ant in each frame. I am growing satisfied with the precision of my accumulation of ants and time as represented by grains of rice, until my postwar Japanese mother finds me and slaps me upside the head for wasting all that rice and tells me to get back inside and do my homework.

Specific Light 1

Someone is in a terrible hurry. Current mode of transport not a car but an airplane, unlikely to go any faster than this. In a terrible hurry and is sitting in a window seat and has very good vision. Is hungry, but makes false sacrifices of food for speed. Tired, but hurried. With very good vision, looks out the window of the mostly white airplane inching across a sky filled with mostly white clouds. In moments of flailingly acute concern, this purportedly very good vision allows for the recognition of a light—a light of that color—reflected off the very black back of an ant, a single ant on the ground, and the ant, too, in it.

Ice Event 2

A colony of ants living under ice. The ants divide into two groups, the Away Ants and the Home Ants. The Undecided Ants consult with the Queen, who advises them to go, naturally.

It is only when the hockey game picks up momentum that the Away Ants begin in earnest the accumulation of ant-heat. In a show of support, the Home Ants muster up some sympathetic heat. Towards the end of the second period, the Away Ants take a deep breath and begin their ascent.

An extraordinary convergence of several elements works to liberate each ant from the thick sheet of ice: the propagation of ant heat which melts an upward path for the ant, the repeated scraping of hockey skates across the uppermost layer of ice, and a massively precise convergence of location and timing not dissimilar in exactitude to that required of hockey goalies.

The goal of the ants who manage to break free from the ice is singular, yet manifold. The immediate task is to traverse the ice rink without being severed by the blade of a passing hockey skate. Once the ant finds its way off the ice, the imminent concerns shift from danger, speed and luck, towards endurance, instinct, speed and luck. They set immediately to the task of climbing to the nether regions of the Indian Peaks Wilderness Area. The distance from the University of Colorado Ice Arena to the trailhead is 22 miles with an elevation increase of 3,500 feet. From the trailhead to the peak, where Bob and Betty Lakes lie quietly waiting, it is 6 miles with another 2,000 feet elevation gain, with a total altitude gain of 5,500 feet.

Here the ants divide into two groups: Old-School Macho Ants, and Contemporary Survivor Ants. The Old-School Macho Ants believe in their physical strength, hardiness and speed—so much so that they plan to make the entire trip on their own with no external help. Most of them die. The Contemporary Survivor Ants, however, assess the situation with speed and accuracy and good explorer ant instincts, and casually crawl up the side of a car that looks as if it is mountain bound. The ants who take hold of the bumper fall off, but those who find that neat crevice where the door meets the body, they manage to stay on for the whole ride up.

And even then, only a fraction of these Contemporary Survivor Ants emerge from their vehicles to find that they are at the right trailhead. As the ants set off upon the trail, they are once again divided, this time into Shameless Hitchhiker Ants and Double Dutch Hater Ants. The Shameless Hitchhiker Ants recognize that even with the good fortune of having received a ride to the correct trailhead, there is still a long ways to go, a longer distance than their bodies could withstand. Some, whose ancestors were pioneers, recall hearing stories about back in the day when they used to hitch rides across the street by hanging onto the shoes of human pedestrians. Or about those ants, the first ants ever to make it all the way across the length of the Great Wall of China.

The Shameless Hitchhiker Ants know that they need the help of a human hiker if they are to make it through this journey alive. And again, the choice of vehicle becomes an all-important decision, as not all human hikers will make it to the top. Some of the Double Dutch Hater Ants try to catch a ride on an abandoned water bottle, or a sole that has fallen off of a worn down boot. The sole goes nowhere without a human foot attached, but the Double Dutch Hater Ants cling on, filled with stupid hope.

At this point, the number of ants remaining who are still on the right track has dwindled considerably. Meanwhile back at home, the Queen in the ice has fallen gravely ill. Fear, panic, and worry are spreading underneath the ice at the thought of life without a queen.

If all goes well, there are a number—not a large number, by any means, but a number still—of ants who make it to the very top. They take a drink of water from Bob or Betty, both of which are fed by the melting glaciers off the continental divide. The surviving Ice Rink Ants are met with a ceremony of dancing marmots, in which the Ice Rink Ants exchange geographical information pheromones with the Glacier Ants. The ceremony culminates in the presentation of a female ant, a pretty young thing by frozen ant standards. The Ice Rink Ants die in exhaustion, their part of the mission having thus been completed. Having been entrusted with the rest of the mission, the Glacier Ants now form a tight ball around the Princess, and set out immediately on their long journey. A marmot representative takes the ant ball to the water's edge, and the whole colony of marmots sees off the ant congregation as it begins its journey downstream.

By the time it reaches town, having dodged numerous dangers and threats and potential calamities, the ant ball has shrunken considerably, having lost many surface ants along the way. With the Princess still tucked away in the center, the ant ball maneuvers its way into the city's water supply in such a way that it travels through the hose that leads to the Zamboni that maintains the University of Colorado Ice Arena, and it is deposited back under the surface of the ice.

The Queen having died a few days earlier, the ant colony is in a state of uncertainty, fear, and general misfortune. Thus a warm, pragmatic welcome is bestowed upon the newly arrived Princess, now Queen, who quickly sets up shop and leads the colony once again into prosperity, and so goes the tale of the survival of the ancient Frozen Ant Species.

Ant Heart

Exists here only due to a misspelling of the word "heat," though the topic of ant heat has already been discussed at great length in other installments. The sad owner of the thus disparaged ant heart comes rushing forward, demanding that it not be implicated in the writing of any tracts regarding sad ants. First of all, nobody said anything about sad ants, to be precise. And secondly, happy ants are so completely out of fashion that the mere mention of the phrase "happy ants" has already and continues to lower the value of this text, faster than it can write itself, faster than the accretion of more words more words more words that are added in a desperate attempt to dilute the effects of the phrase in question.

From the mouth of the ant, a scroll is officiously unrolled, revealing a certain amount of fine print. And if I were more able-visioned, I would be able to make out exactly what those words said—but instead, I am filled with the dreadful knowledge that indeed all the crimes, sacrifices, and inequities of these last few moments are nothing, nothing to speak of, in comparison.

Thank You for the Children

When the earth is on fire, all the ants come running out of their nests and hills and humans and farms and intestines and carrot cakes and ice rinks and hamster cages in a mad panic. Those who were already outside at a picnic also join the panic. The only safe structure nearby is an old abandoned slide, replete with ladder-like steps, a landing at the top, and, of course, the slide. In a well-intentioned effort to escape the fire, the ants parade up to the top of the slide, where they accumulate, at first gradually, then with increasing speed as the word gets out. The ants huddle together on this landing, which is large enough to accommodate a medium-sized child. Although the number of ants that can be accommodated on this landing is fairly substantial, it still fails to meet the needs of the ant community on this tragic day. As more ants arrive, they are forced to pile atop one another, until at some point the surface tension of the mass of ants breaks and they start to slide down in clumps and bundles, clutching one another out of desperation or in search of comfort, slide back down to the wretched earth from which they try to escape once more.

Ant Migration

Under which sheet of white very white paper. Standard issue black ant. Appalled or indifferent or at a standstill, said ant begins to write. With no implement but its own rear end, a trail of food matter taken in on one continent and deposited, in the form of writing, on another. While in transit across the ocean, the ant is otherwise known as cargo, freight, baggage, but never passenger. It shakes its fists in the air, trembling at the accumulated and perceived injustices of its world. And then it arrives, and proceeds to locate a fold of paper. As much like home as anything else, in spite of the fact that it is anything but. Several attempts to crouch, in a singular sturdiness of ant huddle. Beside it, a bottle of lotion or a building. How much longer before food or companionship. How much is necessary in order to accomplish which ant task, such as walking or pheromones. Nothing to panic over, nothing to find peace over, nothing to hate or love or worry over. Still crouching. Paper still paper. Fold still fold. Ant still ant-like, but also beginning to depart from anthood, a whathood for whatgain.

Arranged Insects

I have entered my thirties and my mother is growing increasingly impatient or traditional or both. On the surface she claims she just wants me to be happy, but really we all know that she wants nothing more than to wave around pictures of grandchildren, just like all her friends. And then one fine day, she decides to take matters into her own hands.

I have always known my family to be strangely and, quite frankly, too intensely traditional for my own tastes, but recently the man who married my cousin informs me that they are, well, a number of years behind what you would normally consider traditional. As proof of this, my mother takes the following action, according to some logic that I am too young to fully comprehend. Into a room full of nice young unmarried men, she unleashes a large assortment of insects, and I get to make my decisions based on what happens next—although at this point, all issues of marriage have been set aside, much to everyone's chagrin but mine.

Love

A butterfly grows up on the other side of the bullet train tracks, lulled to sleep each evening by the intermittent swish of a train sliding by. As an adolescent butterfly he is often praised by his coaches and finds himself on the track and field team, which is where he develops his own, special technique for flying. His is a no-flutter, even-flapping technique with a highly developed sense of microcurrents, and soon he is recognized all the world over as a high-speed champion. "He's going to the Butterfly Olympics," the neighbors say to each other as they hear him speed by.

One day he takes some time off from practice to be with his girlfriend, and they spend the day playing in the wake of the passing bullet trains. One way that this story continues is that a beautiful bouquet of flowers lures the girlfriend butterfly inside an open train door just as the door closes and takes off, girlfriend trapped inside. The other way that the story continues is that the girlfriend, having grown sick of her boyfriend's arrogant ways, has already decided that she has had enough of him and that she'd rather start a new life for herself, wherever the train may take her.

In either case, off she goes inside the train, traveling the bullet train at bullet train speeds. The boy butterfly chases after the bullet train with his specially-developed, high-speed flying technique, as only he could do. Any other butterfly would have given up before even starting, but this butterfly has confidence. And more than that, he has love, his true and undying love for his one and only sweetheart. He chases after the train and gives it everything he's got, and then some. Unfortunately the train does not stop for a long, long time. If it is the case that the girlfriend intended to leave him, we are probably slightly relieved to know that he will never know the truth, as he continues his chase after the train, flying faster than any butterfly has ever flown before. If only the Olympic judges could time him now.

As testament to his true and undying love, the butterfly flies after the train for as far as he can, for as long as he can. The definition of this is that by the time he finally stops, he is on the very brink of butterfly death. He can no longer fly, and fades to the ground, landing beside a delicate flower, which he does not see through the tears in his eyes. He shakes his tightly clenched butterfly fists at the sky before exhaling his very last breath.

On the other side of the train tracks, a man is being interviewed.
So, what are your hobbies.
I like to give blood.
You don't say!
Yes, I've done it 106 times so far.

Entrance

Some ants aspire to greatness, some long for a little break, others float peacefully along in a leaf-boat they believe is bound for eternal glory or sweetness. The nouveau-ambitious ants of today, however, aspire to artistic immortality. Japanese ants with such aspirations have been taught since youth that the best way to make their dreams come true would be to find a way to get depicted in the artwork of a promising young student at the Tokyo National University of Fine Arts and Music.

This is not a new idea, however, and word is getting around that these days it is just too competitive to try to get in with an artist by loitering on the college campus. For the last few years, ants have been quietly raiding the entrance exams for the school, hoping to be featured in somebody or other's entrance exam drawing—getting them early, so to speak.

But this whole idea of getting them early is a tough call. These days there are so many young Japanese kids clamoring to get into art school that the campus itself is unable to accommodate the thousands of hopeful applicants all at once. Now they've taken to using the Kokugikan—the place we go to watch our sumo wrestling—as the site of the first round of entrance exams for the Tokyo National University of Fine Arts and Music. And the ants have accordingly made their way there as well.

On the day of the exam, official administrators announce the topic, the artists set to work demonstrating their artistic virtuosity, and the ants parade around that ring of rope, strutting their stuff, hoping to catch somebody's eye, to make it, make it in, get drawn, painted, and eventually regarded with enduring admiration from all the world over.

Which is the story of how we met—or did you mean something else when you asked me that question.

Ants in a Japanese Can

Keep getting hurt, on more counts than one. They are quite crowded inside the can and all of them are in one kind of dangerous situation or another—in fact this life is full of dangers around every corner and rim. The ants near the bottom of the can are in a dangerous position altogether different from the dangerous position near the top of the can. The can is open. The ants are numerous, and are all still inside the can. A few ants clamber up to the rim, but are inevitably cut by the sharp edges of the open can, and after having an appendage or body part sliced by that oh-so-sharp edge, they inevitably fall back down onto the heaving masses of ants inside. The ants at the bottom of the can desperately need the ants at the top of the can to move, preferably out, so that they might get some air, because ants need oxygen too, you know.

So one valiant ant after another valiant ant attempts to make its way past the Sharp Edge as it has come to be called, and one valiant ant after another valiant ant fails, and soon enough, all ants, valiant or not, are dampened under the weight of a large collective sigh. The heaving masses are on the brink of utter despair. Somebody starts worrying about how the species is expected to continue if all ants are either stuck at the bottom of the can, or stuck near the treacherous Sharp Edge. Thankfully, however, this being the unusual kind of day that it is, just at that moment a Japanese-Greek chorus stands up, dropping their olives and pickles to their sides. Linked in a circle all the way around the can, the chorus begins chanting a song that we correctly or incorrectly assume will reveal the solution to all our problems.

Ants in Tokyo

Are crowded very crowded indeed and so they are small very small compared to their countryside relatives and so the small Tokyo ants they communicate with small Tokyo ant sounds like this (   ) and they hear each other quite well, like this (   ), whether it is a panic sound (   ) or a food sound (   ) or a dead bug sound (   ), they can hear each other very well, very well for a species that doesn't have ears. They communicate very gently but quickly and hear each other, all of each other, all the many numbers of each other very often and almost all of the time, except when there is a large Tokyo noise like a truck (truck noise) or a girl screaming (girl scream) or a Western-style symphony (loud orchestra sound) or something equally loud, during which moment the ants cease to hear each other at all, because at first they hear the noise, and then after the noise comes a ringing in the head. And then they begin to hear each other again, as they grow accustomed to this ringing in the head, they gradually begin to hear each other and the vibrations they make upon the waves of the ringings in their heads, the ringing starts to warp and warble a little bit, and that is how they find each other again so that no one has to feel lost for very long at all, no not at all.

Chinese Patriot Ants

So what if they have more 'human' rights elsewhere, they say. So what if they don't spit and shit on the sidewalks. And drive big, beautiful cars full of their big, beautiful family members, they say. They have a lot to say, these ants, and rightfully or not, they are the ones who recognize the implications of everyone's actions upon the larger ecosystem, after all, and understand that taking strong action now could make the 'world' a better 'place' later. Or so they had heard in a lecture given by one of the Chinese Dissident Butterflies.

For a long time, activism was more focused on the efforts to curb emigration out of China into Western countries, but now it is all about resisting the influx of Westerners into China—a veritable invasion, according to certain members of the ant population. To this end, certain sectors of the movement have chosen to use food as the medium of attack (or defense, if you would prefer), in a cross-species attempt to make Chinese food less appealing to the Western palate. Some committees are dedicated to increasing the spiciness levels of many dishes, while others are engaged in an advertising campaign featuring locusts, spiders, and live worms as condiments.

One committee has named itself the Xiaolongbao Task Force, whose mission is to ensure the removal of soup from the soup dumplings which have recently been gaining popularity in North America and certain European countries. In many cities, the work of the ants has been so thorough that the xiaolongbao has come to be dismissed as nothing more special than an ordinary piece of dim sum, thus depriving innocent diners of the knowledge or any concept of soup inside of a dumpling, thus effectively and triumphantly killing any China-bound inclination they may have secretly harbored.

This is how it is explained to me as I discover, for the first time last night, that the original xiaolongbao is in fact the elusive soup dumpling which I had been craving for many years now, and the ant which I discover inside my dumpling is not a mistake, but in fact is part of a large, national campaign to keep me from knowing too much about the riches that await me on my upcoming trip to Shanghai.

Korean Ants Too Erudite for Their Own Good

A particular region in South or North Korea where ants dig ant holes: this much is business as usual.

An entire colony of them, yes it takes an entire colony, one per character, to draw—with the thickness, turns, curves of the passageways—a particular Chinese character, one of the 13,500 of the traditional, non-simplified Chinese characters.

These characters created underground by the nesting ants are consequently only visible from a below-ground, perpendicular-to-the-surface-of-the-earth cross section, meaning they are not visible at all, although whoever needs to know already does know, which is good enough.

Points of reference do exist, however. Highly trained specialists have developed methods for recognizing small convexities in the earth, which indicate the edges of the aforementioned cross sections. And in fact, if one steps away and above the entire scene of such points, the points can be connected in order to form the outlines of yet another traditional Chinese character on the surface of the earth. This character can be said to sum up the entirety of the meanings and intentions behind the aggregate of the underground cross-sectional Chinese characters. Or perhaps the meanings and intentions of an entire civilization of South and North Koreans.

A team of linguists, scientists, historians, and archaeologists are currently working to discover first all of the individual underground characters, with the ultimate goal of discovering the one overarching character formed by their respective points of reference, and have received grants, commissions, and permission from their loved ones to devote an unprecedented amount of time to this project.

The rest of us stay at home eating potato chips and their respective crumbs, waiting for the day when the answer to this question will be indirectly revealed, in the form of a question, on one of the new episodes of *Jeopardy!*

Huge Shadow

Caused by a very low light upon a very small ant, its elongated legs move not slower, just taller, with a weightiness akin to that loaded gun over there on that table. Beside the ant is the trigger, but only in shadow. In shadow the ant meets its lover, angles in for a kiss, passes right through her, unless, perhaps, is devouring her instead.

Lines

A group of ants on an adventure try to spread out and get all over the place, though their intentions are invariably thwarted by instinct and they end up in a line again, a beautiful ant line as if they had never ever strayed, not only from the beautiful ant line that they are now in, a beautiful ant line parallel to a beautiful green line, green line of yarn, and so it is that parallel is beautiful and black becomes green and lines have a natural inclination towards returning, and towards each other.

This particular green line was never trying to stray from its line-like qualities, but was simply taking a temporary stroll away from the scarf from whence it came and the neck around which the scarf was wrapped, had taken a special leap, or a drop, if you will, to explore some fabled place called ground, earth, dirt, to meet up with and have, if lucky, a short affair with a line from another dimension, reach all the way through and beyond the ground and up again towards a warmth and a scarf around perhaps another neck, discover a warmth in the form of this moment, and so it is that lines are at times able to not only conduct but generate warmth and we don't need any pies or soup to prove it, not this time we don't.

Great Love

Two precocious ants harbor an incredibly strong belief in the strength of their love for each other. With much confidence, they decide to embark upon a long-distance relationship, the distance long not in the normal ant scale, but long enough a distance such that it might qualify as a long-distance relationship for humans. Every night the ants go to bed separately, with the smug and satisfying knowledge that they each feel no less love for the other ant than if the distance had been a million miles closer.

Hitchhiking

I was never very good at double dutch, which I am growing keenly aware of as I see that everyone else has already found a ride. We are trying to cross the intersection, but since we're not fast enough to get across while the cars are stopped, we need to get up on a shoe and hitch a ride on someone's foot. A moving foot is tricky, though—you have to jump on at just the right moment, and then quickly get up to a lace or a zipper or buckle or something, anything, to hold on to. And the ride can be rough, depending on how fast the human is traveling, and on what kind of shoes. You better not fall off, is all I know. And so anyway, all the other ants have already gone and I am about to be left behind, no I already *have* been left behind, unless I get on that shoe, no that one, this one, this next one, or that one, oh.

Battle

One hundred gazillion delicate flowers and one hundred gazillion ants get into a chicken fight. There is big money riding on this. The delicate flowers are on each others' backs, but ants, all ants, are already and have long been in the habit of carrying each other, for long distances at that. The height differential between delicate flowers and ants is not compensated for at all, since this is nature we're talking about, where there are never any pretensions of fairness. That said, the ants are big for their species, and the flowers are high-altitude feisties. In the pre-game huddle, the ants debate the merits of the Climbing Up strategy. The vote may be close, but it is a number greater than their capacity for counting, so no agreement is reached before the whistle is blown. A big breeze comes in, the delicate flowers show a bit of sway, a cat walks by and freaks out the ants, and just when it's looking like we're going to be in it for the long haul, the special feature is interrupted by the regular programming, just because we didn't shell out for the Insect Channel pledge drive last month.

Homeowner's Competition

Or, evolution of the floor as an exotic status symbol. That time and place where "floor" means not linoleum, carpet, hardwood, or even dirt, but ants. A bad floor has roughly a 40% mortality rate, most likely due to the additional bad luck of high heels, entertainment centers, and cats. A good floor is extremely well-organized: the uniformity and tightness of the grid can create an ant surface tension of up to 65 dyn/cm^2. All of which is contingent upon the floor having recruited sufficient numbers of ants to begin with. That said, the value of an ant floor depreciates in a sharp slope along the axes of time and wear, while a brand new one can be purchased only on the black market, and only by people who have been carefully screened for ant-corpse allergen sensitivity.

Range of Vision

Sometimes I get all down on myself for the ordinary sort of life I lead. Other times I worry that I don't get enough exercise, and so today I spend the entire day in my own home being an ant. I walk everywhere, especially to all the places that I can't normally get to, and see all kinds of things that I normally wouldn't.

It takes me all day, but I get around. And then pretty soon I feel the need to leave the house, which is how I end up in a ballroom, where accordingly there is a ball going on and people, humans, are dressed in formal attire. I don't really have a handle on women's fashion these days, so I fail to notice who the superstars of the ball are and what they are wearing, and fairly quickly lose interest in the whole thing, which is a shame because far on the other side of the room, there is a woman wearing a lovely low-cut gown, with a black necklace, and I am too far away to see that her necklace is in fact made of a chain of ants, holding on to each other for dear life.

Improvisational Score

This performance may take place over any duration of time, from zero seconds to many many years.

A number of insects are placed in a clear container so that they are as comfortable as possible, given the circumstances. They are given oxygen and food and water, though they may not escape. The container of insects is placed on stage and a light is directed through the container and projected onto a large screen so that the audience may see the insects.

Each musician chooses an insect, and plays accordingly.

If two insects begin fighting, the corresponding musicians should also fight, musically or literally.

If an insect dies, the corresponding musician should also die, musically or literally.

Rain

It begins to rain ants, out of nowhere but the clear cliché of a bright blue sky. We are instantly distraught, confused, and frightened at this new meteorological development, while also wondering how it could be that we all managed to be sick or otherwise absent on that day in school when they teach you about all those foreign cultures and their ceremonies and customs. If we had been at school that day, we would have had no trouble determining, with little to no deliberation, that it must have been one of those species of giants, most likely in the midst of what is the equivalent of a wedding or funeral ceremony, in which the guests throw ants into the air, and we are now starting to relax again, believing we have sorted things out and congratulating ourselves for it, when suddenly we are accosted by a torrent of blue eyeballs and now we really truly do not know how to defend ourselves from them, mentally, physically, and emotionally.

Repatriation of Ants

You can't call it immigration if they are plucked from their homes and transported in a jar on a train to a big city, where they are used, displayed, and exploited for the fact that these country ants are thrice as big as your ordinary Tokyo ants.

My friend starts to wonder if perhaps he has done a Bad Thing when he notices that the ants just aren't eating. He says he is feeding them the exact same thing that he saw them eating back in the country, such as apples, and I tell him that the Tokyo apple might look just like the country apple to him, but perhaps the ants, the ants can tell the difference. Like when I eat Japanese food in the US or in France, they claim they are serving me Japanese food but I know it's not the same. I know how these ants feel. He says he's resorted to basic forms of sugar like honey, and, well, sugar, and even then they won't go near it. I suggest they might be homesick. That's another reason for not wanting to eat.

Time passes. The ants adjust somehow, enough to survive, anyway. Then comes the time when they are no longer needed, and my friend is about to dump them in the neighborhood park. At this point I am exasperated at his lack of sensitivity for—in spite of his apparent interest in—ants. I don't even want to begin trying to explain their predicament—not only are they going to be in a completely new environment all over again, but they haven't had to seek out their own food in ages. And you think some local colony is just going to take them in? There's not a single ant colony in Tokyo whose nests are big enough to accommodate them, and they certainly haven't shrunk down during their stay here, with their exoskeletons and all. They probably don't even remember how to dig—and even if they do, their muscles have probably atrophied beyond repair at this point. Just where did you think they were going to live? How will it even occur to them that they should at the very least huddle together closely for warmth? How will they suffer the humiliation of all those passing ants who will laugh and jeer at them for their enormous size, not to mention the fact that they just can't fit in, or simply fit, anywhere at all? Some of these ants are quite sensitive, and can't even handle being stared at. Who will provide the necessary psychiatric services? Who will teach them the language with which to speak to the psychiatrist?

My friend is staring at me, but I suspect, rather, that there is something behind me he is also staring at, something very large or very small, and on the count of three I am going to duck.

Tomatoes

Very small and at the foot of a large window, I am worried seeing that tomatoes are falling from the sky and landing directly on the ants, except that no one has told me that at the very last moment, out of my frame of vision, the tomatoes turn into red flowers and all the ants are not only safe, but happy.

And the cause of those gently thudding sounds goes unknown, for as long as I can keep track.

Translucent Ant Skin in Spring

Everyone has been hard at work for hours now on the most recent catch, half an orange, I believe, when one single ant emerges out of the ground, at a bit of a distance from the others. All the rest of the ants have been programmed to keep their attention focused on the orange, but I can see it all quite well, the way that particular ant catches the light: the skin of this ant, shiny and youthful, giving the freshly sprouted green leaves on that nearby tree a run for their proverbial money. Now of course I know that there is no such thing as skin on an ant, but trust me, it is truly that glowing and truly that beautiful, not airbrushed nor photoshopped, it's so clear I can almost see right through it, and being the only one who can see it, for that matter, I turn and sigh at the delicate flowers who are slowly turning their backs to me.

Values

A siren is heard—and so it is true, then, that a disaster is approaching this and every neighboring anthill. The ants are instructed to take their valuables and run. Some ants mistake the word "valuables" for "values," but they, too, run. Instead of relating to you some kind of story about ants and their various objects of sentimental value that they pack up into little bundles and take with them as they flee, I am more interested in the ants, a majority of them, in fact, who choose to take each other. There are ants that carry other ants, and ants that get carried. Some ants—fewer, but some—carry each other, and they carry each other.

Ant Breath

Twenty ants are placed in a glass jar, about which they are extremely displeased.

At first they fog up the glass in a state of uneasy panic, but after some time their movements slow down.

One of us with half a heart decides to set the ants free.

The jar is opened, and the ants flee in a mad burst of energy.

The jar is closed again, a sealed, cloudy container still carrying the tortured breath of innocent ants.

Waking Up Under New Rule

I woke up this morning to find that my hands are no smaller or larger than they were last night, but it now happens to be that I can only pick up one thing at a time, ever. If I grab a second object I am rewarded with a swift kick in the ass. From where, I haven't the slightest idea. I was doing just fine at first—glasses, shirt, mug, remote control—but this was before I figured out the new system. Once I knew it, I couldn't resist, and kept looking for the loopholes—a strand of hair, the other arm, part of a blanket. I tried to get used to, and enjoy, the kick in the ass, but I couldn't figure out how to wire it towards the pleasure side of my brain, or how to convince myself that this lack of control was a good thing, though perhaps all this will come with time. I went outside in the hopes that it would inspire me, ran my hands through bushes, picked things up while running, lifted small children with my arms but not my hands. I tried to outrun the kick. Played in a jungle gym full of balls in primary colors. Peeked in through the window of a kickboxing gym. The inevitable end to my dilemma came, of course, when I happened across a colony of ants. I picked one up and let go, as it scurried across my palm. I acquired another, simply by extending my finger to the ground. Another ant crawled aboard, and then another, then another, until I could no longer tell the difference between a kick and an ant.

Thank You

To my parents, my brother, my partner, my children. To my extended family, including Shigeru, Akiko, Eugene's parents. To the institutions that have supported and nourished: Yotsuya Art Studium (esp. Kenjiro Okazaki, Susumu Kihara), UCSD (esp. John Granger), Naropa SWP (esp. Anne Waldman), Bard College, Vermont Studio Center, Santa Fe Art Institute, Tokyo University (esp. Tom Gally, Wakako Kamijo), Komaba chiku hoikujyo. To the editors at Les Figues Press for rounding up these ants (esp. Andrew Wessels, Teresa Carmody). To these peeps: Yelena Gluzman, Kyong-Mi Park, Lisa Samuels, Che Chen, You Nakai, Jen Hofer, Chris Martin (and his ant paintings), Keith and Rosmarie Waldrop, Forrest Gander. To everyone on Facebook who helps me edit at odd hours of the day and night.

To the following people who inspired or instigated some of these texts (in no particular order): Sally Picciotto, Trisha Brown, Patrick Durgin, Che Chen, Chris Martin, Takako Arai, Jill Maio, Matthew Zapruder, Maggie Siegel, Ishikawa-kun, Melody Sumner Carnahan, Naoki Matsumoto, Tony Ko, Marina Abramović and Ulay, Tehching Hsieh, Yoko Ono, Miya Masaoka, Katue Kitasono via John Solt, Rim El Jundi, Jorge Boehringer and a performance of Gayageum, Nobu, C Salt, Aida Sehovic, Jack McLean, You Nakai, Chris Tonelli, Laura Wright, Mayumi Kawaai, Jordan Harrison, Susumu Kihara, Violet Vixa Juno, and George Lewis.

To the editors of the following publications, for publishing earlier or other versions of the ants, in English, Arabic, Spanish, Vietnamese or English-Japanese bilingual form: *6x6, Area Sneaks, Ars Interpres, Blowfish, Cannibal, Conduit, Denver Quarterly, Dusie, Fact-simile Poetry Trading Cards, Fascicle, Filling Station, Friends of the Library Magazine (University of Wisconsin-Madison), Hot Whiskey, Lana Turner, Left Facing Bird, Mandorla, Meena, Mrs. Maybe, New American Writing, Octopus, Out of Nothing, Poor Claudia, RealPoetik, Saltgrass, Sawbuck, Sixth Finch, Sonora Review, Sprung Formal, Tien Ve, Twaddle, Unpleasant Event Schedul*e.

To the editors of the anthologies in which some ants have been included: *The Encyclopedia Project–Vol.2 F-K*; *Kindergarde: Avant-Garde Poems, Plays, Stories, and Songs for Children*; *I'll Drown My Book: Conceptual Writing by Women*; *La alteración del silencio: poesía norteamericana reciente*; *Stranger at Home–American Poetry with an Accent*.

To the editors at Calaveras and Dusie (and the Dusie Kollectiv) for helping spawn three chapbooks: *Insect Country (A)* (Dusie Collective, 2006), *Insect Country (B)* (Dusie Collective, 2007), and *Insect Country (E): Bilingual Insects* (Calaveras, 2012).

INSECT COUNTRY is an ongoing investigation and tutelage under the auspices of the universe as lived by insects, mostly that of the ant variety. Works produced, conducted, performed, committed, or documented thus far include texts, performances, a collaborative book defacement, an open poetry studio, several chapbooks, a podcast, the naming of a non-collective, and various other plans involving film, dance, and music. Collaboration proposals are also welcome.

Some INSECT COUNTRY performances include: *Insect Country C: Insect Orchestra + Wall Installation*, curated by Les Figues Press at LACE (Los Angeles Contemporary Exhibitions) as part of the *Not Content* series; *Insect Country D: Large/Ladybug*, a short film; and *Insect Country F: Structured Improvisation with Dance and Poetry*, performed as part of the Whenever Wherever Festival in 2011.

The ants have been lucky to travel as far and wide as they have, sometimes being performed by others besides myself (this is quite welcome!)—including Pascalle Burton in Brisbane, Michelle Leggott and Helen Sword's Poetry Off the Page class at the University of Auckland, and by George Lewis in the Carnahan/Sumner home in Santa Fe. And on that note: I may not have been able to properly keep track of where all the ants have been—I regret any inadvertent omissions.

To a very large number of people, including many friends I have been lucky to have: if I have anything good or interesting (love, kindness, ants) to contribute to the world, it is because of those same things having been given to me in the first place. Thank you.

Contents

3	We the Heathens	25	Halloween
4	An Ant in the Mouth of Madonna Behind Locked Doors	26	Happy Holidays
		27	Fear of Cold
5	Ladybug	28	Ant Intrusion 1
6	Girl Talk	29	The Cannibal
7	Battery	30	No Collective
8	Ant Farm	31	Anewal
9	Colors	32	Parade
10	Slackers	33	Hazing
11	Apple Speed	34	Sufficient Gravity 1 (Wind)
12	Wall	35	Sufficient Gravity 2 (Slide)
13	Training	36	Sufficient Gravity 3 (The Surface Tension Challenge)
15	Argument	37	Cavities
16	Couch	38	Swimming in the Presence of Lurid Opposition
17	A Linear Night		
18	Capture the Flag	39	Ants in the Wind
19	Harsh Edit	41	Watch
20	Curling	43	What Is an Ant Getting Washed with the Rice?
21	Decay		
22	Carrot Cake	44	Manifold Destinies
23	Desert Ant	45	Ant Liberation
24	Aggregate Heat	47	Sign
		48	Billboard

49	Box with Arms and Butterflies	76	Korean Ants Too Erudite for Their Own Good
50	Chinese Ants on the Wall		
52	Old-Fashioned Messenger Ants	78	Huge Shadow
53	The Ant on the Ship Coming Towards Me	79	Lines
		80	Great Love
54	Ants Preparing to Catch	81	Hitchhiking
55	Ant Shoes	82	Battle
56	Antennae	83	Homeowner's Competition
57	Progress	84	Range of Vision
58	Large	85	Improvisational Score
59	Art Project	86	Rain
60	Specific Light 1	87	Repatriation of Ants
61	Ice Event 2	89	Tomatoes
65	Ant Heart	90	Translucent Ant Skin in Spring
66	Thank You for the Children		
67	Ant Migration	91	Values
68	Arranged Insects	92	Ant Breath
69	Love	93	Waking Up Under New Rule
71	Entrance		
72	Ants in a Japanese Can		
73	Ants in Tokyo		
74	Chinese Patriot Ants		

Sawako Nakayasu writes and translates poetry, and also occasionally creates performances and short films. Her most recent books are *The Ants* (Les Figues, 2014) and a translation of *The Collected Poems of Sagawa Chika* (Canarium Books, 2014). Other books include *Texture Notes* (Letter Machine Editions, 2010), *Hurry Home Honey* (Burning Deck, 2009), and *Mouth: Eats Color – Sagawa Chika Translations, Anti-translations, & Originals*, which is a multilingual work of both original and translated poetry. She has received fellowships from the NEA and PEN, and her own work has been translated into Japanese, Norwegian, Swedish, Arabic, Chinese, and Vietnamese. More information can be found here: http://sawakonakayasu.net.